Otto's Poison Discovery

An Adventure in Home Safety

Jennifer Watson

Illustrated by Ralph Voltz

Written in accordance with the
Central Texas Poison Center at Baylor Scott & White Hospital

BROWN BOOKS KIDS

Otto's Poison Discovery
An Adventure in Home Safety

Publisher's Cataloging-In-Publication Data
Names: Watson, Jennifer, 1982- | Voltz, Ralph, illustrator.
Title: Otto's poison discovery : an adventure in home safety / Jennifer Watson ; illustrated by Ralph Voltz.
Description: Dallas, Texas : Brown Books Kids, [2018] | Includes hands-on activities and a teacher's guide. | "Written in accordance with the Central Texas Poison Center at Baylor Scott & White Hospital." | Interest age level: 005-008. | Summary: "After Otto makes a mistake and uses bathroom cleaner instead of soap to wash his hands, his mom calls poison control, and the man at the poison control center sends Pal, a friend to take Otto on a poison discovery through his home to learn all about how to keep safe from poisons."-- Provided by publisher.
Identifiers: ISBN 978-1-61254-978-1
Subjects: LCSH: Poisons--Safety measures. | Cleaning compounds--Toxicology. | Cleaning compounds--Safety measures. | CYAC: Poisons. | Toxicology.
Classification: LCC RA1214 .W38 2018 | DDC 615.9--dc23

Brown Books Kids
16250 Knoll Trail Drive, Suite 205
Dallas, Texas 75248
www.BrownBooksKids.com
(972) 381-0009

A New Era in Publishing®

ISBN 978-1-61254-978-1
LCCN 2017948840

Printed in the United States
10 9 8 7 6 5 4 3 2 1

For more information or to contact the author, please go to:
www.AuthorJenniferWatson.com
www.PoisonControl.org
www.SW.org/Poison-Center/Poison-Landing

To those who put in a lot of sweat equity in helping make this dream a reality, thank you!

Special thanks to the original illustrator and designer, Benjamin Harper, for all of the hours spent; you were crucial in helping set the foundation for Otto and Pal! Thanks to Ralph Voltz, the new illustrator with an abundance of talent and skill who so beautifully added another layer of life to Otto, Pal, and the book as a whole. In addition, special thanks to the Commission on State Emergency Communications (CSEC), Baylor Scott & White Hospital, and the American Association of Poison Control Centers (AAPCC) for all of the support you provide on a regular basis.

Finally, thank you to the publishing professionals at Brown Books Publishing Group for the personal attention to this project and to me as an author. You have really made me feel like a member of the team!

Introduction

Poison centers across the United States receive millions of calls annually related to various types of poison exposures. About half of all calls involve children six years old and younger. Children are naturally curious, as it is their way of learning about the world around them. Unfortunately, children put almost everything they see and touch in their mouths, even if it does not smell or taste good. Ingestion is the number one method of poisoning in children. Children may also be exposed to poison through their skin and eyes, by breathing it in, or through bites or stings.

Poisonings are classified as injuries, and in order to reduce these injuries in children, the Central Texas Poison Center has created the components in this book to assist you in teaching poison prevention. This program was designed to familiarize you with information about the most common types of poisons, how to poison proof your home, and the importance of the poison control number.

What a Poison Center Does

If you dial 1-800-222-1222, no matter where you are in the United States, a designated regional poison center will answer your call. The people who answer the phones are medical professionals—registered nurses, pharmacists, and/or physicians who have extensive education, training, and expertise in the field of toxicology. With the expert knowledge of the poison center specialists, about 90 percent of poisonings can be treated and managed at home. However, if necessary, the staff may refer callers to the nearest hospital and assist in the person's initial treatment and follow-up care.

Poison centers also have the responsibility of providing public education activities for teachers, students, and citizens, as well as professional educational opportunities for health-care providers. Education activities include special events, presentations, health fair booths, free material distributions, and many more! The main goal of poison center educational activities is to prevent poisonings and to promote awareness of poison center services.

Teacher's Guide

It is recommended that teachers read this story in two sittings. A great stopping place is right before the characters go outside to discover the poisons hiding outdoors.

As you read the story, stop and interact with students.

1. When Otto is washing his hands in the bathroom, point out the label on the bottle. Ask students, "What do you think will happen if he washes his hands with bathroom cleaner?"
2. When Otto's mom comes to help him, ask students, "Have you ever gotten soap in your eyes? What happened when you did?"

3. Otto's mom remembers to call poison control. Ask students, "If your mom isn't home and you need help, what other adult can help you?"
4. There are poisons hiding in the bathroom. Have students name places and things that can be dangerous.
5. Emphasize that medications can help you if you need them but can make you sick if you take them without an adult. Ask students to name some adults who are safe to take medications from.
6. Explain to students that some cleaning supplies can be tricky and look like something safe to drink or use. It is important to ask an adult before touching any cleaning products.
7. Have the students repeat the rule, "Ask an adult before you EAT, TOUCH, or SMELL ANYTHING." Name a few products, and prompt the students to respond, "Ask an adult." For example, say, "You remembered you didn't take your vitamin this morning and want to take it now." Their response: "Ask an adult for help."
8. Call your local poison center at 1-800-222-1222 and ask them to mail you free magnets that you can pass out to your students. As you hand out the magnets to your students, instruct the students to have their parents place the magnets on the refrigerator and to program the number for poison control into their phones.
9. Recite the number with the students several times. Check for understanding by asking them to repeat the number.

Center Activities

Where Poisons Hide:

Using the worksheet, have students color the items that are considered unsafe (e.g., cleaners, medications, makeup, etc.). Next, have students cut and paste items in the locations where they are normally kept in their home. Instruct them to take these sheets home and show them to their parents to discuss poison proofing in their own homes.

Number Recognition:

Using the worksheet, have students color and decorate the poison help number. Ask students to practice writing the number in the spaces provided.

Bubbles / Hand Soap:

Provide safety goggles for students, and allow them to make bubbles with hand soap. Ask them to describe how the bubbles feel and look. Ask them what ways they can stay safe at home or at school while washing their hands.

Call a Specialist:

Post a poison center sticker or magnet in the home center. Encourage students to take turns pretending to dial the poison help number on an inactive phone.

"Otto, wash your hands. Then you may play your discovery game," Otto's mom says.

In the bathroom, Otto rubs his hands, making the soap grow bubblier and bubblier.

"I can make bubbles!"

Otto laughs at
his discovery.

Otto likes how the bubbles crackle when he squeezes them. The more Otto rubs his hands, the bigger the bubbles grow, until—**POP!**

A giant bubble splashes in his face and eyes!

Otto's mother comes quickly when she hears him crying.

"Oh, no! That isn't soap!"

Otto has made a mistake and used bathroom cleaner instead of soap.

Otto's mom starts rinsing his eyes under running water from the faucet.

She remembers Otto's doctor telling her about the poison center. She has the number programmed in her phone.

The specialist at the poison center knows a lot about poisons and staying safe from them.

“Luckily, this was a mild cleaner,” he says. “Otto’s eyes may be a little sore and irritated, but he will be OK. Poisons can be tricky. Can I send my friend Pal to show Otto how to stay safe from poisons?”

“Otto would enjoy that! Thank you,” Otto’s mom replies.

When Pal arrives at Otto's house, he says, "I want to help you stay safe from poisons. Would you like to join me on a poison discovery of your home? Afterward, you will be able to take your family and friends on the discovery, too!"

Otto likes this idea!

"In the bathroom," Pal shows Otto, "poisons can hide in the shower, the cabinets, and even the toilet. Some of the poisons can burn your skin or eyes, while others can make you sick if you drink or sniff them."

"Eww!" Otto cries. "I wouldn't drink out of the toilet, but my dog, Rex, does!"

"Many dogs do, but I am glad you don't!" Pal chuckles.

"In the bathroom,
medications, makeup,
cleaning supplies, and
different kinds of soaps
could harm you. A good
rule to remember, no
matter where you are,
is to ask an adult before
you EAT, TOUCH, or
SMELL ANYTHING."

Pal leads Otto into the kitchen.

"People also keep medications and cleaning supplies in the kitchen," he says. "Medicines can help you if you are sick, but only an adult should give you medicine. Remember to ask an adult before you EAT, TOUCH, or SMELL ANYTHING."

Pal opens the refrigerator for Otto.

"The refrigerator stores food for us to eat. Food can spoil, even in the refrigerator, and then it may not be safe. Medications and drinks that may not be safe for you could also be stored in here. Just remember to ask an adult before taking anything from the refrigerator."

Pal opens the door to Otto's garage.

"The garage is a wide-open space with many kinds of chemicals," he tells Otto. "Ask an adult before you set foot in here."

Pal and Otto look outside. "Would you like to explore outside?" Pal asks Otto.

"Yes! I love going outside, and it is safe from poison!"

"It may be fun, but there can be dangers out here, too," Pal says. "Let's discover some together!"

Pal points to a pile of wood. He puts on his gloves and carefully lifts a log from the pile. Pal explains to Otto that spiders can live in many places, including woodpiles.

He shows Otto a couple of spiders among the logs. “Most spiders are harmless, but some can be dangerous. If you see them, leave them be.”

Pal shows Otto where other creatures could be hiding.

"You can find fire ants inside ant mounds that look like big piles of dirt. They can sting you and leave a little blister on your skin that may itch."
"This guy is called a redheaded centipede. His sting can be very painful."

"A sting from a bee or a wasp can hurt. Stay away from insects, or ask an adult if they are safe to touch."

Pal also explains to Otto that some plants can be harmful to the skin, while others are only harmful if eaten.

"Ask an adult before touching any plants," Pal says.

Pal tells Otto about snakes.

“Snakes in the wild can be dangerous. It is best to stay away from all snakes unless an adult says it is safe. Make sure you wear closed-toed shoes when outside, and if you come across a snake, back away slowly, and get help.”

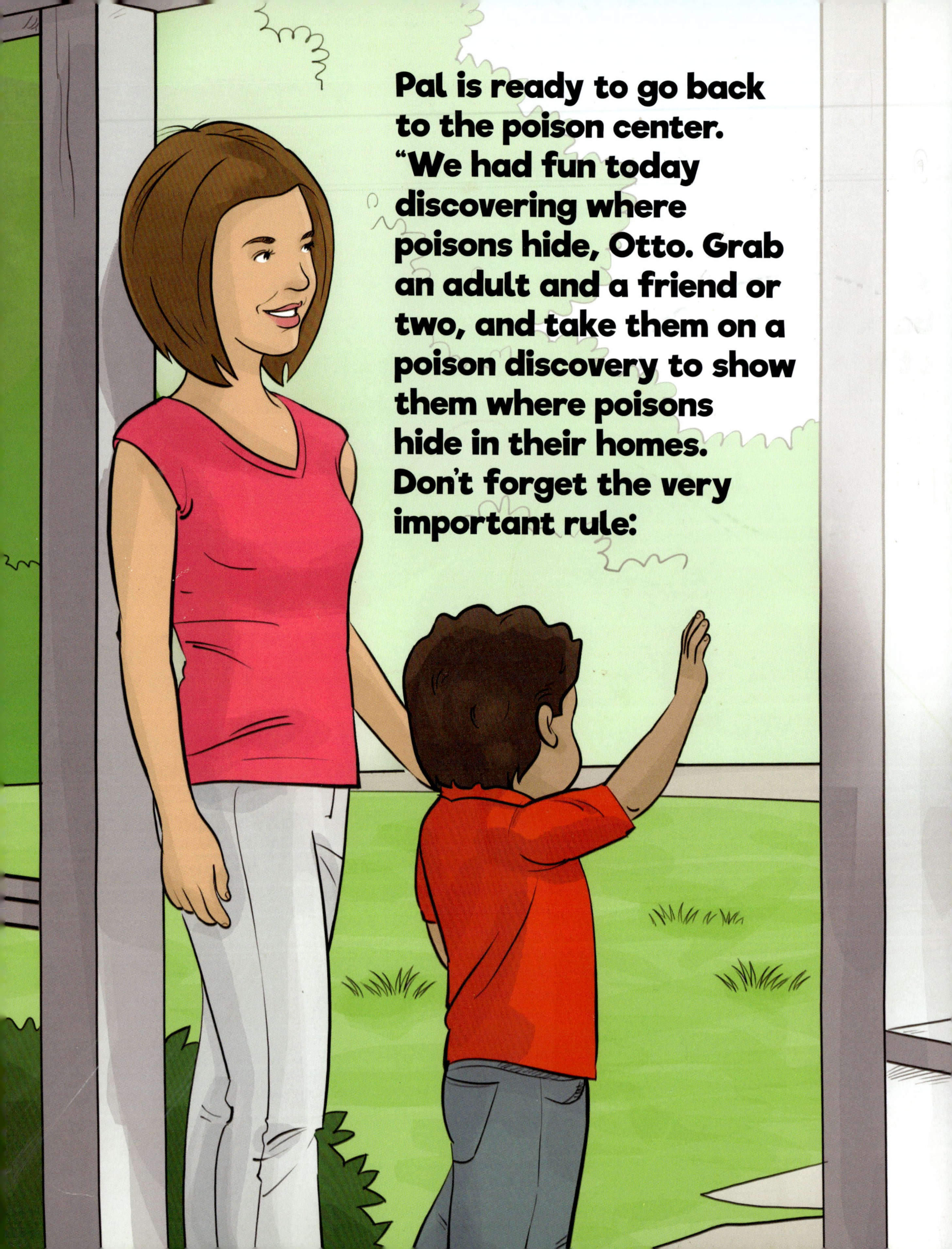

Pal is ready to go back to the poison center. "We had fun today discovering where poisons hide, Otto. Grab an adult and a friend or two, and take them on a poison discovery to show them where poisons hide in their homes. Don't forget the very important rule:

Ask an adult before you EAT, TOUCH, or SMELL <u>ANYTHING</u>."

As Pal leaves, he shouts back to Otto, "Call us at the poison center at 1-800-222-1222 any time, day or night, if you need help or if you have questions."

Poison Discovery in Your Home

Take a walk around your home with your children. Together, see if you can find places where poisons may be hiding. Remind your children of the story and of everything Pal recommends doing to stay safe. Lock away items that may not be safe for your children.

KITCHEN

- Lock away items that could be unsafe for your children, such as cleaners and soaps.
- Place all medicines out of sight and out of reach of your children.
- Install child safety latches (locks) on all drawers or cabinets where you keep cleaners and other chemicals.
- Keep all food items away from cleaners and other chemicals.

LAUNDRY AREA

- Lock away items that could be unsafe for your children. Some unsafe items could be cleaners, soaps, and bleach.
- Keep your laundry products in the container they came in.

BATHROOM

- Throw away old or expired medications. Call your local poison center at 1-800-222-1222 to find out safe ways to dispose of medications.
- Keep your medicines in the containers they came in.
- Lock away items that may be unsafe for children. Some unsafe items could be soaps, makeup, cleaners, and nail polish.

GARAGE/BASEMENT

- We keep many unsafe items in the garage. Teach your child that they should go in the garage only with an adult. Make sure to keep all items you feel may be unsafe locked away from children. Unsafe items could include gas, pesticides, fertilizer, paint, etc.

GENERAL HOUSEHOLD

- Beer and wine beverages can be dangerous to small children. Keep your open drink in your hand or away from a child's reach.
- Keep all cigarettes and items containing nicotine (a chemical in cigarettes) out of reach of children. Nicotine can make a child very sick.

OUTDOORS

- Check for bee and wasp nests and ant mounds often.
- Clean up any piles of stuff and keep the grass cut low to deter snakes and/or spiders.

IN CASE OF A SUSPECTED POISONING

If you suspect your child may have gotten into an item that may be unsafe, ALWAYS:

1. Take the child away from the item or room.
2. Try to see what the product is.
3. Call your poison center right away—even if you are not sure.

Make sure you:

______ Save your local poison center number in your phone: 1-800-222-1222.

______ Teach everyone in your house how to call poison control.

______ Lock away items that you think may not be safe for your child.

Be a poison safety expert!
Garage
Outdoors
Kitchen
Bathroom
Place the pictures of the poisons in the box where that poison can be found at home.

Poison Detective!
Color the items that could be poison.
Rx
answers: nail polish, lipstick, body spray, hand lotion, medicine, eye drops

Number Recognition

Color the number for the poison center:

1-800-222-1222

Trace the number:

1-800-222-1222

Write the number:

1-800-222-1222

About the Author

The Central Texas Poison Center (CTPC), located at Baylor Scott & White Hospital in Temple, Texas, has been helping the public with poison exposures, prevention, and information for more than twenty years. The CTPC is part of the Texas Poison Center Network (TPCN) and a member of the American Association of Poison Control Centers (AAPCC). Poison centers provide free treatment advice to the public regarding poisoning. They are staffed 24-7 by medical professionals trained in toxicology, and they answer more than thirty thousand calls per year in the CTPC region and more than two hundred thousand in the state of Texas. The CTPC educator creates activities, programs, publications, and more to educate the public on the services of the poison center and on staying safe from poisons. The education department provides free presentations and materials to the public with the mission of preventing poisonings and promoting the services of the poison center.

Jennifer Watson, an educator and writer living in Central Texas with her husband, four children, three dogs, and two cats, began educating the community in 2012 when she started working with the Central Texas Poison Center. Seeing the need to reach more people and facing limited funding, she created this book to help educate the public on the dangers of poisons. Having found her true passion in writing, she resigned from the poison center to pursue her writing career. However, the poison center still has a highly qualified educator on staff, and Jennifer is still available for book signings and public presentations.